Perfectly Imb

Roger Strotz

Day 1

Miro

Thud. Thud. Thud I can only hear the beating of my heart. It deafens the sounds that we normally hear and yet rarely take a moment to listen to, the faint whistle of the wind, the quiet blustering of leaves. *Thud. Thud. Thud* My consciousness is asleep. My mind is blank. Although my eyes are wide open with dilated pupils from the recent thrill, I am blind. I cannot coherently perceive my surroundings, which have been heavily tainted by my deed. *Thud. Thud. Thud* My mind fails to perform the simplest of recognition functions; to transform the biting cold upon my bare skin to that of numbness and pain it should cause. It does not even register the very core thing that is the cause of this sudden paralysis of consciousness, as if it were weightless within my hand.

As abruptly as a line of coke would jump start the mind into action after inhalation, my mind clears like an unexpected defiant ray of sunlight breaking through a mass of stormy clouds. The icy air ripples through my body causing it to shudder. I observe the landscape. A sea of glistening whiteness lays before me. The surrounding haunting trees stripped of their leaves by this merciless never-ending winter add to the feeling of isolation and loneliness. Was this not the precise reason why I chose this destination? To be safe from prying eyes? This instantaneously jolts my mind to my last memories of her. Her piercing sapphire blue eyes. No! I cannot think of this. I will not turn to see the results of my endeavours. Not at this crucial moment! I continue to struggle to straighten by tangled thoughts and only achieve in doing so by relaxing my clenched fists and dropping the knife. I need to leave this place. I slowly begin to walk back from whence I came. The snow beneath my feet, which the blood has now soaked, crunches pleasantly under my footsteps.

Bevic

"Stupid. Stupid. Stupid little man. Oh, I know what's a great idea, let's try and bury it in the freezing rock-solid ground. Yeah, great fucking idea Bevic, very well thought through." They say the first sign of madness is talking to yourself. Perhaps then, I might be a genius, for just as the saying goes; in every genius there is a touch of madness. But if I am such a genius, why on earth did I come up with this stupid halfwit brain-dead senseless plan! I must look so ridiculous in my board shorts and my delightful blue Hawaiian shirt clawing at this god forsaken snow-covered frozen earth. "Ahh, I am not getting anywhere." I need to calm myself down. What did Dr Serdnic always say, "deep breaths through the nose and out through the mouth" …. That's better. I need to pause, regather my thoughts, and work out how I am going to bury this green wonderful, dreamy, delirium-inducing amount of cash. Oh, how beautiful you are! Soon enough I will utilise your perfect four edges to find myself on a warm crystal white sandy beach soaking up the sun's cancerous powerful rays, whilst sipping a cool refreshing mojito that comes with its own cute little yellow umbrella. "Snap out of it Bevic." I need to concentrate! I need to soften this ground but how? Ah ha, maybe I could use my spit? Wait no, even better, I can perform one of man's most satisfying functions. "Ahh." I can feel the warmness radiate against my skin. Oh, what comfort it brings to pee. That's done the trick! I will have this concealed in no time. Maybe I am genius.

This return leg seems to be considerably longer and colder than I remember or is it simply that the adrenaline from the earlier exhilarating events has finally been overwhelmed from the extensive period of exposure of this skin attacking, small dick causing ice cold weather. Oh, how powerful our natural survival instincts are? No matter how much I resist, my lips tremble, my arms shake, and my chest pulsates. Oh, how we - wait! Are those voices I hear? Indeed, they are the familiar yet currently unwanted noise of two people conversing. "Shit. Shit. Shit." What should I do?! I won't let them see me! I won't let them find my darling money! I need to get out of sight. I need to lie down! Damn, the wetness has already started seeping through the bare clothes I have on. I raise my head slightly in the deep snow and scan the surface like a submarine periscope poking its head just above sea level. A young couple, 30 meters or so away, are standing to my right, in a small opening of trees. The wind must have carried their voices deceiving their closeness to myself. What are they doing out here in this wilderness?! All over my body starts to ache and scream in pain as if surrounded by thousands of little knives puncturing my skin's surface and then slowly being driven deeper and deeper. I will not give in to this god forsaken sub-zero snow. This money is mine! I can feel that my will is on the verge of breaking! But wait, as I now closely observe the couple everything seems to have stopped or more accurately stated, slowed down. It so delicately and graciously sailed through the air as if he were a performer proving his skill and brilliance to his audience. An audience that solely consisted of myself.

Only the reflection of light from its edges betrayed its true identity and purpose to me. The resulting blood seemed to dance and hang in the air like an orchestrated ballet, with the knife acting as the conductor's baton commanding with its touch each blood droplet elegantly cascading from her smooth neck. As the composition ends, as is regular to do so, the conductor turns to his audience and seems to bow in wait of the expected appreciation following such a spectacular event. This particular performance, however, is not followed by the rapture of applause but instead a curtain of deathly silence draws over this final scene. I cannot move! My body is paralysed but why? Is it due to the horror that's been played out before me, or simply the recognition of a familiar face in such a desolate area?

Miro

I eventually reach the white Vauxhall that blends naturally within the snowy surroundings where it remains stationary and unchanged. Huh, unchanged? It's in these moments one can truly appreciate how insignificant life is, how the spectacular events following my earlier exit from this very car has had no effect on its functionality. Although this discovery on its own is not surprising, when drawing comparisons to my previous thoughts and those of others that the loss or taking of a life would cause the world to collapse around them, it is rather striking and noteworthy.

As I reach my front door after the forty-minute ride back into town and six flights of stairs, a veil of tiredness descends over me. Upon entering my small one room flat the single bed that nestles tightly within two corners of the concrete room entices me with its facade of cosiness. I stumble a meter or two to reach the bed and exasperated from fatigue I collapse on it. Sleep has taken me.

I wake with a sense of achievement and embodied in power. And what power it is to be able to dictate one's life with such ease. Others may say "I wish you were dead" or "I'll kill you," but unlike these often-spoken false claims of power, I have proven my mental strength and resilience to perfectly execute a well-defined plan and make these statements a reality. I see now that my previous exposure of this emotion, the chopping of wood with an axe or the shooting of a glass bottle with a 9mm pistol was but a glimpse of what this rare sensation could offer. Like a man that has just faced and survived his greatest fear, I feel invincible, as if possessed by God himself. How many others have become masters of their destiny, completely unperturbed by the ambiguity of the life which lays before them? I and only I can live life fruitfully in the knowledge that no individual will ever have control over me. Unlike the common man who is like a puppet, listening and doing exactly what is demanded of him by their employers, parents, lovers, there are no strings attached to me. I am beyond all doubt free, not restrained by the invisible constraints that society enforces onto an individual, commanding how one needs to act and live. Parallel to a bird that has broken its chains of captivity and flying high in the sky, I can now see all that surrounds me, and I am above all others. Even now, as I think back and re-live the moment I can once again feel the energy and power surge through my veins. I delicately clasp my gloved fingers around the knife's wooden handle. As she turns to me, I can easily conclude from her gentle relaxed facial features she has not yet observed the deadly item held down alongside my right leg. We gaze deeply into each other's eyes and momentarily I lose my concentration of the task at hand. The black long woollen jacket which comes down to her ankle's flutters silently in the wind. A slightly stronger breeze causes a few strands of her striking light blonde shoulder length hair to waver across her delicate face. She tucks these stray strands back behind her petite ears to once again reveal her pale white skin and alluring eyes. Ironically, the sudden realisation of the beauty of her glistening sapphire blue eyes and the acknowledgment of the magnificence of human life, I am jolted back to reality and reminded of what needs to be done. My eyes must have betrayed my thoughts and intensions for as the period of silence extended her face altered from one portraying minor amusement to confusion, and lastly fear. It's within this instance when her face contorts to this final emotion of fear, I can sense the strength flow from my feet all the way to my head. I can feel it in every muscle, in every cell, in every single fibre that makes up my body. I am invincible. I am ready. I tighten my grip and raise my right arm across my chest, so that my right hand is level with my left shoulder as practised. Then in one smooth calculated motion I slice horizontally left to right. As I watch the life drain from her sorrow filled blue eyes, even before her body falls to the snow, I instinctively turn and stare at the redness below me. As I replay this spectacle in my head, just as when the act was performed, I feel overcome with tiredness. The adrenaline and energy have now drained from within me, and a sense of weariness has deceased over me. Sleep has taken me again.

Bevic

Praise God! He is walking away into the treeline! He is no longer within my perception. I need to get up! I need to get out of here! But wait, the money. Surely upon the discovery of the body and the following crime scene investigation they will identify my footprints in the surrounding area that will inevitably lead them directly to it. It's too high risk, I must retrieve the cash and keep it with me thereby ensuring its complete security. No one will take it away from me! It's mine Goddamn it!

Although I have re-salvaged my prized possession and now within the comfort of my piece of shit car, just as the sun is inevitably losing its daily battle to the night, my body is on the edge of shutting down. "Come on baby, don't let me down now." I temporarily close my eyes as if in some sort of prayer and turn the ignition. "Goddamn useless piece of junk!" Why are you not starting?! "Oh, come on baby, don't do this to me, not now." I whisper willingly to her. I turn the key again. I take a deep breath and sigh in relief as the beautiful machine-like purring sound of a running engine fills my ears. "Aw baby, thank you!" I shout in relief as I slap the dashboard with delight.

After a painfully slow fifty-minute drive caused by having to concentrate wholeheartedly to drive in a smooth manner due to the uncontrollable shaking of my numb cold arms, I arrive at my flat complex. "Oh shit." Only now as I park in front of my greyish grubby apartment block, next to my neighbour's white Vauxhall, does the realisation of the danger I have put myself in by coming back here finally materialise. Whilst I was completely focused on the money and its safety, I had given little thought to the risk of my own life being so close to a stone-cold calculated killer. Can I really sleep in a room next to the murderer within this grimy narrow flat complex on the top floor that is only occupied by the two of us?! But I can hardly move from exhaustion and my body is screaming for sleep. For tonight my place will have to do! At least I can rest easy in the knowledge that the money will be close to me and secure.

As I weakly crawl up the sixth flight of stairs using my left hand to push off each step and my right hand to hold the briefcase as I did on the previous flights, my head starts to feel woozy, and I am overcome by a coughing fit. I only succeed in flopping over the final step onto the subsequent corridor before the darkness engulfs me.

Solamov

As sure as the rising of the sun Dmitry Solamov's alarm rings at 5:00am as it has been doing every morning for the last elven years since he became a detective. Although he is always awake before this alarm only after 3 beeps have sounded does he casually extend his arm out of the bed to turn off the device as per routine. Solamov then jumps into the shower. He does not take enjoyment from the warmth the water provides. He simply perceives bathing as a necessary task in the maintenance of the human body. Detective Solamov is a strong believer that for one to serve justice correctly one can only do so with a clean body and clear mind. Following the drying of himself, he takes a moment to observe himself in the mirror. The man looking back at him is one with chestnut brown hair and a recently clean shaven face that compliments his sharp short haircut. Solamov stares intensely into this man's deep dark, almost black, brown eyes that. He can sense the air of confidence and self-belief that radiates from the man before him. Solamov then proceeds to put on a freshly dry-cleaned light grey suit, a well ironed white shirt and black tie. Before leaving his home, as is customary, he does a final check with the man in the mirror. As he does so, he acknowledges, as he does every day, that he is ready to serve justice and will do so whatever the circumstances or costs. For ever since the murder of his parents when he was eight, he has vowed that he will restore balance within the world by ensuring that those that have sinned will be held accountable for their actions.

Solamov arrives at the crime scene later that same afternoon and is approached by two police officers, of which one of them is unknown to him. The unknown officer immediately identifies himself as a new recruit by demonstrating his unfamiliarity with Solamov's practices, which the others have become accustomed to. As soon as the officer begins to utter "The body was found B-" the detective wordlessly raises his index finger to his lips to signify silence, shakes his head, and subsequently proceeds past the stunned officer. The startled officer turns to his partner for an explanation, who then follows to provide one.

"Detective Solamov is a very particular man you know. He does not want to learn any information from a crime until he has made an initial assessment himself and generated his own suspicions of what had occurred. Funny, right? It's something to do with the fact that if information can be gained first hand, then it should be done so to avoid the potential misinterpretation of information received second hand."

The amateur officer, still recovering from shock, simply responds "Tut, does he think we are idiots or something and can't communicate?!"

Solamov strides to the body, crouches and observes the victim. He is instantly astounded at the girl's beauty and youth. No more than twenty-five years of age he thinks to himself. He further acknowledges the whole scene with the striking contrasting colours of the maroon blood, the light blue tint of her skin, the glistening blondness of her hair, the dark black garments, and the gleaming white snow would be rather picturesque if not ruined by the fact that it involved the loss of a human life. She looks strangely peaceful to him, lying there so silently, never to say another word again. Upon closer analysis of the corpse and the immediate surrounding area it becomes glaringly obvious to him, due to the lack of any visible marks of resistance and such a clean cut through her throat, that this was a calculated killing. Rage starts to build within Solamov as every part of his body tenses and his fists clench tightly. He now fully understands that she must of have been allured out here on false pretences and murdered. This was not a killing in a moment of weakness, in a moment of anger. This was a meticulously planned cold hearted execution. An act of pure evil. Solamov senses a sour taste within his mouth from the disgust he now feels. He nods and declares to himself in that very moment that he will find the son of a bitch who was responsible for this and bring justice to him if it's the last thing he ever does. Solamov, who is still visibly frustrated then rises and advances towards the same two officers he encountered ten minutes before on his arrival. "You," as he gestures to the now visibly nervous new recruit "go-head and give me the run down." A moment of silence elapses before the officer is able to regain his courage to speak.

"No personal identification was found on the victim, and it is currently unknown how long the body has been out here, but it was found by an old woman walking her dog at around ten past two this afternoon. She was rather startled when -"

"Where is she now?" Solamov abruptly interrupts with the anger still pulsing through his veins.

The officer only has the bravery to lift one of his shaking arms and point with his finger in the direction of the road behind the detective. Solamov does not turn to look but instead simply motions the officer to continue.

"A single clean cut to the throat." Stutters the officer before carrying on more confidently "She was dragged to this opening of trees and then killed."

"Incorrect!" barks Solamov. "She was not 'dragged' or forced out here. She arrived here at this location in control and with no indication of knowing of what was soon to befall her. If you had even an ounce of intelligence you could have established this simple fact from the indents within the snow, which evidently show two distinct footprints leading to the body with no sign of a struggle. It is therefore clear that the killer and the victim knew each other to an extent. What is yet unclear to me, and is very worrying indeed, is how such an incompetent individual like yourself has managed to get into this police department?!" Solamov pauses briefly to let this settle into the young, inexperienced, and now very much frightened officer's mind. "Find out everything you can about the girl. Who she is, when she was last seen, where she lives, what her hobbies are, and even what her Goddamn favourite colour is! And when you found out, make sure that I find out! Understood?" Without hesitation and not waiting for a response from the two officers, Solamov turns and begins to march back to his car.

Day 2

Miro

I am woken by a sound. In a lethargic state I look at my worn-out leather wristwatch. It confirms, as expected, that it is early morning; 05:56:17AM precisely. I observe closely how the delicate third hand ticks away, slowly counting the seconds up to a minute. Slowly, as if by the mere act of being aware of the passing time, does it seem to run wearily on. Contrary to this, when concentrated on a specific task at hand or in the presence of good company, time appears to quicken in pace; making it almost unbelievable that each minute is comprised from the very same seconds that now tick idly by. But the wonders of time seem to me not only to be constricted to minutes, or even hours. For at the beginning of every year I reflect what is to become in the long years ahead and yet I am fully mindful that those that have passed have done so, so swiftly. Whereby months appear to merge into one and it becomes an impossibility to separate the uniqueness of each individual week, let alone each day. Presently I cannot help to think that minds distortion to the passage of time goes beyond this and is somehow deeply connected to an individual's feelings and thoughts at any one instant. The experience of spinning out of control on a road in my car just over a year ago, springs to mind. When in a complete state of fear and shock I perceived all that surrounded me in state of slow motion with every key detail subconsciously retained for future memory; the hot summer parched air, the piercing screech of the tires, the g-force propulsion of my body into the driver's door, the seemingly steady spinning environment around me, a row of thick knee height hedges that hug either side of the road and act as a border to the yellow rape seed fields that stretch into the horizon in both directions. What purpose could this intense memory serve? Other than enabling me to relive the horror in such clarity and making every hair on my arms stand on end, I am unsure. But the mind's complexity and trickery extends. For how when in a complete state of sorrow and grief, such as in the case following a destruction of a relationship or loss of a loved one does time painfully slow causing the distress to last even longer than necessary. Minutes turn into hours. Hours into days and before long a whole week has passed where the afflicted have lived in a complete cocoon state of self-thought whilst life continues to revolve around them as normal. In those first few days and weeks following a tragic impactful event, things that once seemed so important now do not. No longer does one feel the pressure from work or any other responsibilities they may have. They start to become completely careless of any social norms that one should adhere to, such as, whilst with a group of friends that lively chat away, they sit there silently, truly lost within their own mind. It all becomes so unimportant, and, in that moment, it all seems so meaningless. And yet, time really does heal. For as fast as a blink of an eye, the normality of life returns. One day again they will feel the stress of the job they occupy. One day again they will become irritated by that friend or colleague that talks too much. Time and life go on.

My trail of thoughts become interrupted by the very same noise that initially awoke me from my slumber. The sound resembles that of a harsh cough, but it is its closeness that arouses my curiosity the most. It is as if it were stationary right out-side my door, which would be a very strange thing indeed when considering that only I and my elusive neighbour reside on this top floor. I impulsively step out of bed and head towards the door whilst still wearing the same cloths that I fell asleep in the night before. Upon slowly opening the door and peering out into the tiny corridor my body is instantly filled with a burst of adrenaline from observing the sight that is before me. I instinctively step towards the shaking beach dressed body of my neighbour. I kneel beside his pale white face and by using the back of my hand I touch his forehead. It confirms my initial suspicions from laying my eyes on him, he has a fever and is in urgent need of treatment or a hospital.

As though he could read my thoughts, he simply utters with eyes still closed "No. No. No. please, do not take me fucking anywhere!"

"You need a hospital. You may die in your current state" I whisper in concern.

"I might as well be dead if I leave!" He pronounces, as he momentarily opens his glazed over eyes. They take no interest in me but instead stare intently at the briefcase by the dying man's side prior to quickly shutting them again. Before he can speak further his whole-body shudders into a coughing episode and then only the faint sound of his breathing can be heard.

As if the judgment of another person's life in such a short space of time would be too draining of a task to complete, my mind automatically concedes to the fact that I will honour his wishes. I proceed to find his door keys within his short pockets and successfully drag and lift him into his own bed. I struggle but achieve in removing the few wet clothes he has on and then subsequently cover his body with a few old tattered rugs found underneath the bed.

As I stare down at this man's sorry state of affairs, I cannot help but feel sympathy and empathy. How can this be? How is it possible that the same man that less than 24 hours ago brutally killed in the exact same clothes he now has on, can feel such humility and compassion to someone they barely knew? To have such a desire to help an individual in need. I cannot prevent these feelings that are now overwhelming me, bringing me to my knees and making me shake uncontrollably. So strong they are it is as if it were part of my very make up, inherited from those before me. It must be an integral part of us, the human race, to be so caring and altruistic to another of our kind. The simple acknowledgment that I, a murderer, can feel as I do in this very moment is but a testament to this. It is now clear to me. We are all good and yet we are all evil. It's merely dependent on the circumstances that surrounds us that dictates which one we reside on at any one moment. But wait, is this correct? Can it really be that our actions are purely products of our environments? For if this is the case, then should any man ever be sentenced to death for the sins he has committed? For surely given the right environment this man may have become or yet still has opportunity to become a saint and saviour. Or is it not so simple, and is it instead dependent on the crime itself? Would a more horrendous crime warrant the death penalty more? And would this outlook change if I was the one responsible for ending that person's life? For example, could I pull the trigger on a known child rapist if given the opportunity and would I be right in doing so? But where is the line drawn and who can make such a judgment to decide someone's fate? To determine that someone's existence is no longer worthy and is therefore better off dead than alive? To ultimately destroy the beauty of a life with all its unique hopes, experiences, and memories into a soulless still corpse?! No. No man has the right to do so! Oh God! Forgive me! What have I done?!

Bevic

"Cough, Cough." Ah my fucking head kills and my body hurts like shit on this hard-cold floor. Why on earth am I on the floor and not in bed? "Cough, Cough, Cough." It's all suddenly coming back to me; I was walking up the final few steps to my apartment before I started coughing uncontrollably. I must have blacked out. No wonder my body feels like it has been run over by a ten-tonne truck lying for hours on this concrete corridor surface. I can tell however I had no choice. For even now, although I have such a desire to get up and be in the cosy comfort of my bed, I cannot seem to move. My body is just too week. Ah shit, is that footsteps I can hear? Where's the money?! I have got to make absolutely sure that I am not separated from it, otherwise it would all be so meaningless! It would have all been for nothing! The door to my left squeaks open. I can sense that a stranger has knelt by my side as my pace begins to quicken. I need to let him know that he cannot take me away! He cannot take me away from MY money! "No. No. No. please! Do not take me fucking anywhere."

The stranger softly responds, "You need a hospital. You may die in your current state."

Goddamn it, "I might as well be dead if I leave!"
I only have the strength to quickly flash open my eyes in search of the briefcase; luckily, it is right beside me. "Cough, Cough, Cough, Cough."

Ah my head hurts. The only thing overpowering its sense of haziness, is a banging headache that resembles the continuous and rapid hammering of hammer against a metal plate. To add, my body feels so feeble, it is as if the very thought of ever walking again is but a dream. At least I can take some relief in the familiar soft, lightly buoyant mattress under me. From the shear comfort it brings, its undeniable that I am in my own bed. It's the sort of comfort one can only get from one's own bed. But damn, how did I get here from the corridor. I must have passed out again. I need energy.

I slowly open my eyes, which take a moment to become accustomed to the lack of light. It is already dark. The whole day has gone by in a blur; periodically dropping in and out of consciousness. I begin to make out the room laid out before; the heartless bare concrete walls that enclose me and the little window at the base of the bed, which provides as much light into the room now as it would do in the day. As I turn my head sideways to face into the single room flat, I can just about recognise the wooden door opposite, three meters away, and next to it my beloved overused sink. Oh, what a sink it is. Not only does it deliver refreshing cool drinkable water that I can use to rinse food or wash my hair but it's also a perfect place to piss. Well, it's definitely better than going two floors down to the shared bathroom at least. Ah pissing, what a satisfying activity to undertake. Mm, yet I can't quite remember when I did it last. When was it? Of course, it was in the snow when I was hiding the MONEY!! Come on eyes, focus! Where is it?! Even on its side I recognise the briefcase. Thank God we are still together and only an arm's reach away from one another! Oh, what relief it brings knowing that all the lying, cheating, and stealing have not been a waste. Wait a moment, I can clearly see something on top of my precious briefcase. A cup, next to a plate, with some sort of food on it. Food! I barely manage to lift and stretch out my weary arm to reach the now recognisable piece of bread on the plate but do succeed in doing so. I take a bite of the soft bread and instantly my whole body seems to loosen and relax. I subconsciously grab the cup on top of the briefcase and begin to gulp down the lukewarm tea. Oh, what sweet refreshment this is? Which servant of God has provided me with such heavenly pleasures? Which angel, for the person responsible must be some sort of angel to take such care of a stranger? To remove my drenched clothes, cover me in the warmth of my rugs, and carry me from the freezing solid corridor. But wait, this is no angel, this is the fucking devil; for only now can I re-call the face that was observing me so sympathetically in my lethargic state this morning in the corridor. The killer. The stone hearted mother fucker. Can this really be?

Solamov

It was early evening the day after the body was found when Detective Solamov received a call from the forensic team. It was a short call with a few simple facts, but its importance and impact to Solamov and his investigation cannot be contested. "The victim is Anna Fedorov. Twenty-three years of age. She still lived with her parents on 89 ***** Street. No marks of a struggle were found on the body, and she was dead between 5-10 hours before she was found. She died from a single uniform one and half inch cut along the throat and died within seconds." The detective is currently replaying this one-way conversation within his mind as he drives towards the victim's residence. "Anna Fedorov" utters Solamov quietly whilst shaking his head at the same time. He tightens his grip around the steering wheel in frustration. He acknowledges as he always does, how when a body is given a name, the implications of what has happened becomes even more real and harder to grasp and accept. The detective further understands that he now must begin the all too familiar painful journey of getting to know someone whilst they remain silent and dead. In the end, he will have learnt all there is to learn of Anna; her childhood, her old friends, what she used to like and dislike, what her aspirations were and so on. It is this fact of only knowing the past and not knowing what she would have become in the future that will torture Solamov for the years to come. He is all too aware of this fact for he has been carrying this very burden from all his previous cases, which are the root of many of his sleepless nights. The detective nowadays acknowledges that this is just part of the job and if you are not able to build those intimate connections with the victim, to understand their movements and thought processes, you can also not succeed in capturing their perpetrators.

Solamov reaches the residence and parks alongside the footpath on the road. He turns off the ignition, leans his head back on to the seat and closes his eyes. He takes one deep breath in and out. This, unsurprisingly, is the most difficult part of his occupation. No matter how many times he has performed this distressing task or will do, he knows it will never get easier. To inform parents, siblings, or partners that their loved ones are lost forever; never to cry, speak or smile again. That the person they created, looked after, or were planning their future with have been taken from this world. If the admission of losing someone dear to you is not agonizing enough, to then be told that this person's life was stolen by an act of evil. That someone actively decided to kill and stop the existence of a loved one. There are just no conceivable words that would effectively relay the heart-rending feelings one experiences upon initially hearing this. Solamov, however, always recognises, for it happens to him too, that it is this realisation that the loss of life was through a murder that ultimately causes the predominating emotion of those impacted by the death to change from a deep indescribable sorrow to a profound inexpressible anger and the need to have justice.

Solamov walks up the small gravel path that separates the front lawn equally into two, up to the door of a quaint slightly run-down white bungalow. He gently knocks the pale brown wooden door and waits in anticipation. The door opens to reveal a middle-aged woman, who's striking similarities to the victim; blonde shoulder length hair, pale skin, blues eyes, momentarily stuns the detective as Anna's corpse flashes to the front of his mind. "Maya Fedorov?"

"Yes?" replies the woman inquisitively with a smile. She is somewhat relieved that her boring standard evening may now have some excitement in store.

"I am detective Dmitry Solamov." Any presence of joy instantly vanishes from Maya as she crosses her arms.

"What's this regarding?"

"It's about your daughter Anna. It would be better if I came inside. Can I?"

Maya doesn't seem to have heard the detectives request, as she responds with a heavy undertone of worry "Is she in trouble? Is, is she okay?" A couple of seconds pass as Solamov's silence answers the question. Maya enfolds her arms and brings her left hand over her mouth as her eyes begin to water.

"There is no easy way to say this, Anna is no longer with us. Sorry." As the words resonate within Maya she starts to cry irrepressibly.

"No, No, No. Oh My baby! My beautiful baby! Oh, how has this come to be? How?!" she screams wildly as the tears stream down her face.

"She was murdered, I'm so sorry."

"NOOOOO!" wails Maya in despair as she collapses into the detective's arms and continues to howl in distress. A heart rendering minute goes by. Still within Solamov's arms, "You promise me, you promise me right now that you will find who did this to my baby. And you make sure they are brought to justice for what they have done." She draws slightly away, her watery eyes filled with a mixture of rage and sorrow "Promise me?!"

"I promise."

Day 3

Miro

Sapphire Blue Eyes! I suddenly wake up frightened! As though a noose were tightening around my neck I struggle to breath. The deadly parched air causes me to almost choke as my lungs desperately attempt to draw in more oxygen. In response, my heart beats profusely as if every beat were to be its last. Will these be the last?! The thought hangs delicately in my mind, as my temples begin pulsating violently. An unnatural force starts to build within my eye sockets and almost renders the use of their occupants. To oppose this, I futilely gaze at my surroundings in a delirious like state. I now feel entombed by the four walls that enclose me so closely, rather than comforted by their familiarity. Sapphire Blue Eyes! Once again, they flash to the front of my thoughts. It is as though they were now forever etched within my mind; to be a continuous reminder of what I have done. What have I DONE?! Oh god! Please! Please forgive me?! Never have I felt such agony, such heart ache, such guilt. Surely this is greater than any physical pain one can inflict on oneself. To be in complete state of powerlessness. In knowing I cannot undo what I have done. No matter how much I desire to. I cannot go back and extinguish those initial thoughts that gave fire to my devious actions. I cannot go back and not slice open her neck causing the crimson blood to seep out on the snowy white canvas. Or stand, idly by, while she slowly suffocated from her own blood right before me. What the fuck have I done?! And why, why for God's sake did I do it? It's all so unclear now as my thoughts begin to quicken. Was it simply to see whether I was capable of feeling emotion? To have what so many others seemingly have with ease and yet which has repeatedly escaped me; to have feeling and passion for something or someone. Is that what has led me to this treacherous path?! To see whether my heart was more than just physically present. To see whether I could feel anything?! And was I really convinced by my foolish thoughts that the only way to elicit such a response would be to force myself into performing an incredible act? Could that really have been it? Oh, how truly fucking stupid of me? For I do feel. I feel the deepest form of pain that can surely exist in this world. It feels like my soul is being torn in all directions, whilst simultaneously burning as though alight. It is as if I am experiencing the very horror Dante portrayed of the seventh circle of hell. In attempt to replace the mental pain surging through my consciousness, I start to claw at my skin viciously. The physical agony soars and yet my mind remains true. It only thinks and feels regret and self-deprecation. Sapphire blue eyes! "Ahh GET OUT OF MY HEAD!" Even now as I keep aggressively slapping the palms of my hands against my temples and try to pull out my hair, the image reappears. My eyes begin to burn with soreness from clenching them shut so tightly in hope of forcing away the memory. This must be hell, to be forever at the mercy of one's own thoughts. Normally we embrace the creative and free thinking of our consciousness but it's now seemingly uncontrollable nature simply appears to be a tool to torture me. All other thoughts or concerns that commonly occupy my life and which I now attempt to force into my consciousness appear so irrelevant as my mind stays determined to focus only on the dreadful deed I have performed. Maybe I should take matters in my own hands. Make these tormenting thoughts cease. Make it all stop. And would it not be deservedly so for me to die? I should get out of bed to rid myself from these dark thoughts.

Upon doing so I cannot help but stand motionless with my whole body tensed. Every hair upon my body stands on end. I sense a warm fluid escape my hands as my fists clench further and my nails pierce the skin giving release to the warm blood within. I automatically paced towards my sink and look into the mirror above it. I do not recognise the man looking back. The stranger runs one of his now slightly bloody shaking hands across his mouth and then upwards to his forehead as he uncontrollably begins to sob and shake. The image before me starts to distort as the flow of tears obstruct my vision. I become overwhelmed with the deepest of sorrows and I cannot coherently remember the last 30 seconds; it's all a blur. I need to get a hold of myself and wipe away these tears. I close my eyes and start to take in deep slow breaths. With each breath, the cool air tingles the back of my throat, before continuing downwards to expand my lung cavities. It then proceeds to slowly rise back through my air passages and out my nose. The moment seems to last for eternity.

As I sense that I have regained some self-control, I slowly reopen my eyes to confront the man staring back at me. Isn't it odd that relative to those that frequently surround and interact with you throughout your life, your face is always more of a stranger to yourself than it is to them? Them, who observe it so constantly rather than fleetingly in mirrors ever so often. Them, who know how your face is displayed as your specific facial muscles subconsciously tense and relax to give an outsider an accurate perception of the emotion you are experiencing at any particular moment. But the man before me seems to be drained of all emotion and even any life as he stands there so still. He is now more of a stranger than he has ever been to me. What have I become? Will this be how I will remain? Will I now walk through life as a living corpse, forever struggling to come to terms with the crime I have committed? To go on with this soulless body and, now more than ever, have no understanding of the purpose of life? The purpose of my life. Maybe I should end it all now. Escape from this path of unknown ambiguity. No! I suddenly sense a level of passion and energy build within in me. It will not be so! I will not condemn my life to one where the magnificence of the cells that make up my very being are wasted so prematurely! Or even enslave them to form part of a zombie-like-human that eventually results into nothing but dust! I cannot and will not end my life whilst in the knowledge that I still have the strength to go on. I still have the capability to do good. To bring some sort of meaning to my life though the actions I can take in helping others and making them value theirs. I must find redemption, for otherwise, I will surely only find solitude through death.

Solamov

"Sir?" Solamov looks up from the newspaper article titled '500,000 cash goes missing from Charity Organisation' and acknowledges the young officer from the day before standing in front of his desk. The young man looks dead ahead and without any associated emotion begins to reel off his findings. "As requested, Anna Fedorov is a student of 23 years of age studying philosophy at Royal**** University. She was last seen with a fellow course student, Miroslav Malkin, with whom she has been known to have increasingly more interactions with recently." The officer pauses temporarily and then continues to add, "Miroslav resides at ******* apartment complex on the sixth and top floor, flat number 112." Still looking ahead, he waits patiently in anticipation of Solamov's response.

Solamov nods a couple of times and firmly says: "Maybe there is some hope for you after all. What's your name officer?"

The officer now finally turns his head to Solamov to meet his eyes and replies "Luca Stepurin, Sir."

"That is all Luca, good day." Luca walks away pleased in knowing that he has performed well. For he is fully aware that a man like Solamov, just like a stern father that is finally proud of his eldest son, he can only provide positive recognition in the form of a solid nod. A half smile plays out across Solamov's face as he watches Luca leave before continuing with his afternoon break and resuming where he left off in the newspaper article. Upon finishing the story Solamov leans back into his chair in a state of bewilderment and wonders to himself; what sort of individual would steal from an Orphan Charity and by doing so destroying the lives of so many vulnerable children. Who has such a distorted moral compass he ponders further. Still baffled, he stands up, puts on his grey suit jacket that is hanging at the back of his chair and makes his way towards the parking lot. He enters his saloon black Skoda, and after initiating the leather seat heating, he starts up the inbuilt sat navigation and inputs "****** apartment complex."

Bevic & Miro

Shit! Someone is opening the door. Pretend to be asleep. I hear faint footsteps, as the intruder slowly creeps towards me. Shit. Shit. Shit. He must be right over me. All of a sudden, my sense of smell is awoken and any anxiety that was building within me vanishes immediately. A creamy spiced broccoli flavour hangs in the air and blesses my nose with its scents. It's truly remarkable. Never has there been such pleasure within my nostril passageways that now automatically draw in more of a surrounding aromatic air in an attempt to further enhance this experience of exhilaration. The urge to understand its source is just too overwhelming. As I slowly open my eyes, luck is on my side; my neighbour and now so-called guest, has his back turned away from me. I carefully grab the bowl of soup and the accompanying spoon that has been laid out by my side and take a mouthful of the creamy rich thick soup. Oh, what sweet heaven is this? The divine peppered broccoli soup playfully ignites my tastes buds and causes a sudden intense craving to eat more. Its almost perfect smoothness caresses my coarse dry throat, bringing a much-desired comfort. I can't bel-

"It's my mother's recipe." He says with his back to me. I momentarily pause whilst in the process of taking another spoonful as he speaks these words before slowly continuing to enjoy the next mouthful. Maybe if I stay silent, he will just leave and let me relish this in peace. It's impossible, every spoonful seems to taste better than the last! Damn, he is one good cook; just a shame that he is also a killer. Well, I guess, just like the saying goes, "you can't be good at everything." Wait, I just assumed that all killing is bad. Maybe he is actually a very good killer. What does that even mean Bevic? Why am I even thinking about this stuff?!

*

"My mother used to make it every Sunday as a treat. She used to always say 'broccolis are like mini trees. Trees grow tall and strong, and so will you upon eating this broccoli soup'." Not sure why I am stating this useless information. I initially think it may be a subconscious nurturing tactic that a human might find it comforting to hear another human voice, but I can quickly reject this idea in the full understanding that I am doing it for my own benefit. It's calming me down and lets me keep a hold of myself and reality. I turn to face him on the bed and plainly add "I also brought some fresh tea with me" as I slightly raise the pot of tea in my left hand before placing it down on the floor beside the bed. He simply stares back at me, nods ever so slightly with a fake, almost mocking, small smile. I can sense a feeling of concern radiate from him, as he tensely resumes eating. Why should he be concerned? Not only have I rescued him from the bare corridor but have also provided him with food and fluid to keep him going. Perhaps it is simply due to the fact that he has rarely interacted with me, a stranger. That has been helping him with no easily recognisable motive and is now standing idly by in his room. I should probably leave and let him be at ease.

*

Wow what a freak; telling me that we are some sort of growing tree. Maybe he's a nut case. That might explain the killing. Shit, maybe he feeds them before he kills them as some sort of sick joke. Like a last supper kind of deal. To be fair, if this was my last meal then it's a pretty amazing one to end on. I am probably best just carrying on eating and enjoying it while I can and then if he does happen to kill me at least I will die with a delightful taste in my mouth. I can definitely imagine worse ways of dying. But wait, I don't want to die. This sudden realisation slaps me hard in my face and the fact that I am currently so close to the very thing that could be the death of me strikes further terror within me. I don't want to die; just please let me be. Please spare me. Oh Yes! As if he's heard my very prayers, he's moving towards the door. How brilliant?! *Knock. Knock. Knock*

Bevic, Miro, & Solamov

What the fuck is going on? Although the knocking is actually at my neighbour's door not mine, no one ever comes to the sixth floor. My guest has mirroring thoughts to mine, as he simply turns to me with a face of pure bewilderment. I shrug in response as we continue to stupidly stare at each other with inquisitive faces as if trying to portray the question 'who can that possibly be?' My guest seems to be stuck in some sort of trance; unsure whether to go and find an answer to this intriguing question. *Knock. Knock. Knock*

Now really what the fuck is going?! Why is someone knocking on my door? I am definitely not expecting anybody; I am not even meant to still be here! Before I have time to raise my concerns to my now even more baffled neighbour, he turns the handle and opens the door. My vision of the unexpected knocking individual is obstructed by my neighbour.

"Gooday Sir, do you know where I may find your neighbour, Miroslav Malkin?" I can hear a firm male voice from the corridor. 'Gooday Sir', already sounds like a prick. Ah Miro?! That's it, I can now recall seeing it on his letter box in the foray area when I check every day to see if I have received anything, which I undoubtedly never do. No. 112 – Miroslav Malkin.

"I am Miroslav Malkin. How can I help you" Miro responds almost willingly. What is Miro playing at?! What kind of killer is this?!

"I am detective Dmitry Solamov and investigating the death of Anna Fedorov." Ah shit, this is great! Firstly, a murderer that for unexplainable reasons has been nursing me through a fever, who could have easily killed me at any point in my weakened state; and now a detective, who, if he finds the money and its source, could lock me up for eternity. Can this situation actually get any worse?!

"Oh, that's shocking. How very sad. Please come in detective. I am currently looking after my neighbour who has come down with a severe illness." You got to be fucking kidding me?! Why on earth has he invited him in and especially into an apartment that doesn't even belong to him?! How is Miro even answering so calmly without a hint of concern of his own association with the killing? I on the other hand instinctively swallow, my heart rate quickens, and I can start to feel sweat dripping down from my forehead. Miro steps aside to allow the detective to enter, who does so in a stride. The detective sniggers a touch as he observes the bland one room apartment and then faces forwards to speak to me directly.

"Sorry for the intrusion, I can see from your profuse sweating that you are unwell, but this shouldn't take long." Wow, he said that without any sign of sympathy. Why if I am going to get arrested, does it have to be by a top-class nob? The detective moves to stand towards the foot of the bed whilst Miro leans with hands in pockets against the wall opposite to the detective, close to my head. The three of us form a sort of cross with the door; with the detective one side, Miro the other, and my bed opposite the door. And in the centre of us all is my briefcase and my freakin' MONEY!

*

The detective's face seems to be fixed with determination as every part of him emits confidence, from his firm voice to his overly structured body movements. This man is obviously well experienced in the cat and mouse game that is crime and punishment. It is apparent from his self-assured attitude, that he is the man that regularly finds himself on the winning side of this game with many of his losing opponents justifiably finding themselves behind bars for the rest of their lives. Should I just concede defeat now and confess my wrong doings; for surely, I deserve to be locked up for taking the life out those beautiful sapphire blue eyes? But wait, wouldn't this waylay me of my chosen course; to now do good and redeem myself. For if I were to become caged within a jail, there would be no chance in being able to fulfil this right-doing. I just need to stay calm and hopefully by casually leaning back on this wall I will be seen as such. But something is worrying me more than my own ability to be perceived as relaxed. My so-called patient now seems extremely tense and nervous. I keep catching him glancing at the briefcase as if it were a very young child of his that on no circumstances should be let out of his sight for worry of its safety. This brings back a memory of the day before in the corridor where his sole interest whilst lying half dead was again the briefcase. What could it possibly contain to be of such great importance to a man that is so visibly suffering from a life-threatening fever? Whatever the contents may be, it's definitely the cause of his current uneasiness.

*

The room stays silent for slightly longer than is custom in a social environment and an atmosphere of awkwardness starts to creep in. Before the awkwardness builds to a level that is unbearable, Detective Solamov continues his investigation.

"You studied together with Mrs Fedorov, correct?" commands Solamov sharply to Miroslav.

"That is correct. We both study Philosophy." Responds Miroslav readily with more information than necessary in attempt to demonstrate cooperation and support of the investigation.

"Now more precisely said, 'studied'." Says Solamov almost pleased with himself for identifying this required correction. If Solamov wasn't as distracted as he was by his own praising, he would have easily noticed Miroslav visibly swallowing. "Would you say you were close?"

Miroslav considers the question momentarily before answering "Maybe not close, but two months ago we were assigned a university project together and from then we have steadily started to get to know each other."

"What was the project regarding?" The detective notices that Miroslav's face changes to one displaying surprise for he was not expecting such question. Before replying Miroslav takes his now clammy hands out of his pockets and places them behind himself in an effort to hide the fact that they have begun to shake with nervousness. This sign bypasses the detective. However, from Bevic's viewpoint if he turns his head, which he does so, it is clearly seen.

"The project we were given was titled 'Identify and understand the certain mind set attributes required for one sane human to kill another and how these factors may have contributed to man's evolution and the modern world today'." It's now the detective's turn to display astonishment, who even slightly shakes his head in disbelief with what has just been said by the only suspect of this investigation so far. As Detective Solamov digests this newly attained information, he begins to stare intensely with increased suspicion at Miroslav bringing further discomfort to him.

"Mr Malkin where were you two days ago between the times of 10am to 16:00pm?" queries Solamov with a hint of disgust. Other than the formation of a small layer of sweat on his top lip, Miroslav refrains from showing any sign of panic.

"I was here all day."

"Can anybody vouch for this, Mr Malkin?" Miroslav starts to feel hot under the collar and steps away from the wall in an attempt to cool down slightly. A further moment passes as Miroslav contemplates how best to answer this question and the detective begins to move his hands towards his gun holster.

"I can." Utters Bevic softly. Both standing men in a synchronised manner turn to Bevic, almost shocked by his presence. They were so whole heartedly consumed in their conversation with one another, they had completely forgotten the dying man in whose apartment they currently find themselves in. "The morning of two days ago I became ill, and Miro has been taking care of me since then." Adds Bevic weakly.

Detective Solamov proceeds to rotate back to Miroslav in search of some sort of confirmation, which Miroslav follows to give one.

"It's true." Miroslav responds with a nod and newly gained confidence. Although, the detective cannot yet draw out a reason why the ill man would lie, he is unconvinced with Miroslav's conviction. He knows in his gut he is the man. He is the man that lured out that young woman into wilderness and then proceeded to brutally slaughter her. Anger starts to swell within Solamov. He knows he is staring into the eyes of the murderer. Before he becomes overcome with rage and takes physical action, which he will only later regret, sense intervenes as suddenly as a flick of a switch would turn on a light. Sense reminds him that he must not simply rely on hunches and instead must gather more evidence to build a case to show this man for what he really is. A Killer.

"Thank you for your time, Mr Malkin. I will be in touch." abruptly informs Solamov as he unexpectedly exits the room, which has now considerably darkened as the day has progressed into evening. The two remaining men, the patient and the killer, both intently watch the detective leave before turning to another. Silence fills the air as the two men lethargically gaze at each other and undergo a series of emotions. Firstly, and experienced equally strong by both, is a sense of relief resulting in a smile playing across each of their faces. This is shortly followed by Miroslav displaying puzzlement, which Bevic then reciprocates. The two men then conclude this surreal interaction between themselves by both feeling the same intense emotion of fear. Fear from one another.

Miro & Bevic

Oh, the liberation. The hefty weight of concern that has been resting on my shoulders in the last half an hour has vanished. So close was I to a life of imprisonment; forever caged like an animal. Trapped, with only my torturing thoughts keeping me company and persistently reminding me that I will never be able to lead the life that I now much desire. A life of redemption. I cannot believe it, I am free! And it's all thanks to him, a man I barely know. But why did he lie for me? What are his motives? The pieces just don't add up. Yes, I rescued his shaking body from the freezing corridor, but that would not justify lying to the law and thereby risking accusation of his own association with my crime? The lie isn't even justifiable from my nurturing of him; like providing him with homemade soup this morning, which he oddly enough seemed to be concerned about. Wait! I must have been caught in the moment, for only now as I retrospectively look back do I realise that it was not concern that I sensed from him. It was fear. Fear of me, as if my very presence was a threat to his safety. He must know. He must know that I killed her. But how does he know? Did he see me; was he also out there in the wilderness?! It would explain why he was so chilly with the bare cloths I found him in. But then again, if he does know, what cause did he have to speak out and lie in an attempt to get the detective out of here? What is he hiding? The briefcase! I can only logically conclude that the implications of owning the contents within the briefcase is worse than the potential risk of now being affiliated with a murder. What is within it and what is the man before me capable of? Is now my safety at risk?!

*

Yeah, come on! I feel so alive and free. I'm free! Nothing can describe this feeling. It's as though I have just gotten away with crime. Wait, on hold on Bevic, that is exactly what I have done! Well at least for now and by getting the detective out of here I bought myself some time. On the next available opportunity, I will leave this hell hole of a place, take my money and be on course for a life of relaxation and pleasure. I can hardly wait with the excitement. To have acted and spoken out was the right choice Bevic. It was a good plan. Even seems to have been a good plan for Miro, who seems to be revelling in the fact that he is currently off-the-hook. But wait, why is Miro's face swiftly changing to one portraying confusion? I can almost hear his thinking gears tick into motion, as he is undoubtedly asking himself questions for which he is struggling to answer. Why is he looking so inquisitively at me, as if I were the core to his confusion? It's as if I was a modern piece of art and he a novice bystander artist trying to figure out my purpose and meaning. Dread now seems to be the predominant emotion expressed by Miro. What can he possibly be thinking about and how can it be so important that it has distracted him from the fact he has effectively just got away with murder due to me?! Holy Shit! He must know that I know!! Oh man, oh man, I am screwed. As I see it, he only has two potential choices: either hope and trust that I won't speak out against him, like I just did, or heaven forbid make sure that the opportunity and possibility to do so could not even arise. From how I see it, if I was him, I wouldn't take the risk: dead people don't talk. I am truly fuc. "Cough, cough, cough, cough, cough, cough." Ah this is it, it's over, my final few seconds as he slowly steps towards me. This is the end of Bevic. "Cough, cough, cough, cough."

Solamov

Solamov enters the restaurant and is immediately recognised by the young black suited waiter who naturally proceeds to guide Solamov to his usual table residing in the corner of the large room. As is typical within this esteemed establishment at this time in the evening, his table is the only one unoccupied. Although the detective seems out of place among the other elegantly clad guests that compliment well the low hanging chandeliers and polished wooden tables, the restaurant always has his table reserved. He is after all their most regular, and therefore, best customer; even though he never comes accompanied. The detective is thinking these exact same thoughts himself as he tastes the smooth chianti the waiter has just delivered. Always alone, he thinks. Not married, no kids, no girlfriend. He cannot even recall any sort of relationship within his life that could be constituted as a serious one. He ponders, as he often does, whether he will be alone forever and struggles to comprehend if this bothers him if it were to become reality. It is not that he doesn't want to love or feel loved; it is simply that it has alluded him to-date and therefore he contends its existence. What actually is love, he begins to wonder. It is sought after by so many, but why? Is the common perception that it gives purpose to life and provides the experiencing person with an indescribable sense of happiness true? Just as he frequently does, Solamov now fights an internal battle with himself to establish whether love is real or is simply a fragment of the human imagination to give mankind an aim and meaning to life where otherwise there may be none. Maybe one day he will make a decision on this matter he thinks to himself as he stares at the empty chair opposite, which only further enhances his sense of solitude.

Twenty minutes pass, during which time a second glass of wine is poured for the detective. As he swirls the wine, the twirling deep redness causes Dmitry Solamov to wince in discomfort as the memories from his childhood are reactivated. Dark red clearly defined shoe prints leading from the parent's room lay before young Solamov as he finally gains the courage to step into wood laden corridor. All the ear-piercing screaming have now ceased. No more does the cries of anguish fill the air. "Mum?! Dad?!" His whimpered calls go unanswered. "Mum?! Dad?! You there?" He yells louder. But still only silence greets him. He pauses for a moment to take a closer look at the blood prints before him. The sudden realisation of what they are causes his body to cower in fear, for it was only the other day when he himself leaked the same fluid upon accidently cutting himself. He remembers how the pain shot through his body then. Someone is hurt he concludes. Tears begin to flow down Solamov's cheeks as he becomes unsure what to do. Mummy was always the one that helped him when the red fluid came out and caused him pain. The young boy, the child, decides that he needs to make sure mummy and daddy are okay. From years of playing the hero with his toys, he can now truly become one. Solamov slowly begins to edge towards his parent's closed room door with his back against the wall in care not to disrupt the red prints in the middle. He finally reaches the door and puts his ear against it. Silence. Nothing can be heard. He turns the knob and opens the door slightly. Through the small emerging gap, bright blood splatters across the cream walls can be seen by the young detective. He begins to whine and whimper as he pushes the door fully open. Before him, his parent's bodies lay sprawled out. They lay still. Dark crimson pools surround them. Solamov instinctively goes towards his mother and puts his arms around her back, almost laying completely on top of her. "Mummy, you okay? Come on get up now" He whispers in deluded hope that mummy is only playing and, in a moment, everything is going to go back to normal; soon she will be cuddling and laughing with him again. But she does not stir. She remains silent and dead. In a final attempt the young boy pushes both of his hands repeatedly into his mother's side and yelps "Mummy?! Mummy?!" His futile actions are only interrupted by his own realisation that he has become wet all over. He pushes himself onto his knees and looks down to inspect his top and hands. Red. All is blood red. The detective physically shakes his head in an attempt to remove the memories and by doing so succeeds in exiting the trance he had found himself in. He proceeds to empty his wine glass and indicates to the waiter that a further helping is in order.

As the detective takes a sip from his third newly filled wine glass, he reflects on the events from the last three days and the investigation. He raises a closed fist to his mouth as he struggles to focus and analyses the information attained so far. He acknowledges to himself that if he was fully concentrated on the task at hand, he may have quickly and logically been able to establish his next steps to progress the investigation further. Instead, the interaction with the victim's mother, Maya, arises repeatedly to the forefront of his mind. What a rookie mistake, he contemplates; to have promised a promise that he may not be able to keep. He clenches his fist. Previously he had a clear understanding and acceptance of the emotional toll the job and the impact of failing to solve a death would have on him. Now, this once clear set strategy had become muddied and unclear. For he cannot even imagine what would become of himself if he were to fail and break the promise made to Maya, the mother of a murdered daughter. It weighs heavy on his heart for he fully appreciates that if he does not fulfil this promise the guilt may eat him up inside forever and he may never recover, professionally or emotionally. No, he screams inside his head whilst simultaneously banging his fist down onto the table; causing nearby seated customers to gaze in his direction. He vows to himself that he cannot and will not fail Anna in death nor in providing Maya with the all-important closure she requires. He will rightfully condemn the murderer for his sins. He will rightfully condemn Miroslav Malkin.

Day 4

Solamov

Solamov turns in irritation as the alarm sounds at exactly 5:00am. He tiredly reaches out his arm to stop the infuriating noise and in doing so shoves his phone off and down the back of the bed side table. It was a restless night for the detective with thoughts from the investigation relentlessly playing on his mind. Wearily, he lifts his heavy legs off onto the floor and resumes a sitting position on the edge of the bed. With his hands on his thighs and head drooped, he sighs heavily until proceeding to stand up and slumps into the bathroom. Solamov turns on the cold tap and by using his hands splashes his face three times with the cool water in an attempt to awaken himself fully. Water droplets, taken by gravity, slowly drip down his face onto the floor below as he begins to observe through semi-closed eyes the man in the mirror. Two days of stubble have grown unhindered. The detective knows a shave is in order. He sleepily closes his eyes for a few seconds before reopening them to gaze at the razor by his sink. He shakes his head and decides to instead re-enter the bedroom. Languidly, he starts to gather and re-wear his suit and shirt, which were left as they were from the night before; spewed across the floor. As a finishing touch he loosely ties his tie around his now slightly stained collar, before starring with downcast eyes at the man in the mirror. He looks like a broken man he contemplates to himself. The memories of the thoughts that kept him awake throughout the night suddenly remind him of the immediate task at hand. He straightens his spine and with a half-hearted nod he re-acknowledges that he will not fail in having justice. He decides he needs to go back where all this madness started before any interaction with the suspected murder. Before any promises were ever made. Back to square one. Back to the crime scene.

An ambulance siren startles the detective as he reaches the signs designating the edge of the city. With a quick glance at the rear mirror and the flashing lights, Solamov decelerates and turns slightly so that his wheels kiss the grass neighbouring the road to allow ample room for the emergency vehicle to bypass. The detective than carries on as usual but only a few minutes later does he have to roll the car to a stop at a crossroad and weigh up his options. The road to the left, which is by far the quickest route to the crime scene, has become closed off. With squinting eyes, the detective can make out the flashing lights of an ambulance in the distance, which only helps in confirming his suspicions of the cause of the blocked path. A sarcastic smile plays across the detective face. He cannot believe his rotten form of luck. Should he drive back to the city or go dead ahead in the knowledge that he would have to approach the crime scene from an alternate direction. This he knows would add at least half an hour both ways to his journey. In the detective's mind however, there is realistically only one choice of action. He puts his car into gear and proceeds forwards.

Upon reaching a small parking lot Solamov exits the warm comfort of the car only to be confronted by the harsh cold winter wind. The detective does yet still lift his head up to the skies in appreciation. For as he observes the path that lays before him, he is thankful for the very little snow fallen in the last few days and thus the fact that he does not have to wade tirelessly through the snow. Instead, he can use a set of footprints clearly visible that so happen to point in the general direction of the crime scene.

After ten minutes of walking the detective can finally make out the all too familiar yellow police tape that encircles a crime scene. As his guiding footprints start to angle to the right and away from the opening of trees where the murder took place the detective halts. He turns and looks back down the path he has just undertaken and temporarily becomes lost in his thoughts. What are the chances that these separate footprints have led him almost directly back to the crime scene he wonders? He immediately feels a surge of energy and excitement as he thinks that this surely cannot be a coincidence. He twists back and with a new injection of life and follows the same prints onwards. His eyes move eagerly side to side, scanning and searching for a plausible explanation. The detective only manages to proceed five meters before stopping again at another point of interest. He crouches and inspects the unnatural break within the course of the footprints. An area of around two meters of snow is completely flattened down before the prints seem to recontinue. Whist remaining crouched the detective rotates his head to the left. From this viewpoint he has an almost perfect sight of the crime scene. He then looks down again at the flattened area of snow around his feet. Then back again to his left. He suddenly stands up with pupils fully dilated and clenches his fits as the realisation finally hits him; there was a third person present who lay here and witnessed the murder unfold. It does not take the now fully revitalised detective to logically join the dots. It was the dying man whose apartment he found himself in just the day before that saw this tragedy. Solamov entirely understands that the ill man is now key to the investigation and by persuading him to testify against Miroslav, some justice can be brought to this world. But why hasn't the sick man not already approached police or spoken out whilst in his presence he wonders further? A jumble of ideas pop around in Solamov's mind as he attempts to search for the most rational explanation. Until he settles on one which seems most likely to him; the man feels or is threatened by the suspect in question. "Goddammit." The detective condemns out loud as he finally grasps the gravity of the situation. The only witness that will quickly end this case is currently sick and trapped in his own apartment by the killer who is probably reframing from providing any of the much-required treatment that the poorly man needs. If the ill man dies, then so does his investigation and any hope he had in keeping his promise. Instinctively Solamov plunges his right hand into his right pocket in search of his phone, but instead only succeeds in pulling out his car keys. "Shit!" He sighs heavily as he vaguely recollects knocking his phone onto the floor in his sleepily state this morning. The detective remains stationary as he starts to scratch his jaw stubble and assesses his choices. He reflects that he would lose a considerable amount of time retrieving his phone or even going to the police station directly on the other side of the city. The detective decides he cannot prolong any further the time the ill man has without attention given to his health. He cannot risk losing this witness and with it any chance of keeping the pledges he has made to himself and Maya. He turns and begins to pace quickly back to the car before breaking into a full out sprint to reach it as soon as humanly possible.

Miro

I step out into the open air and a cool gentle breeze caresses my cheeks inoculating new life into my body and soul. I am free and feel reborn as if my senses and eyes have been opened for the very first time. All that surrounds me now seems so novel and wonderful. The trees that lay on either side of this road no longer seem to disappear into the background of the ever-moving picture that is life. They now seem magnificent and almost statuesque as they stand powerfully there with their bare arms stretched out undeterred by the harsh cold weather. Even if they were to lose an arm or two, these impressive giants would forever strive to continue to survive. Oh, how magnificent the living is? Yet still I have barely but scratched the surface of my new intrigue into life with little thought yet given to that of the human body. Even now as I walk, no thought is required to perform this most complex of functions. How can this be? How can life be so self-functioning? I try now to focus on all the intricate distinct elements and the specific sequence of events required to accomplish a single step. The slight push off the ground with the toes from one foot causing a small but noticeable extra tension within the standing leg. The rotation of the knee within its joint bending the leg into two before the leg swings elegantly forwards and with almost perfect precision the foot re-finds the stable surface. Oh, how truly amazing it is that we do not just crumble upon each step into a ball of flesh. It is as though I have finally achieved the ability to appreciate every part of the body without having it subjected to injury first. Never have I felt so gracious and blessed to be alive. I cannot help but break into a stride, jump, and throw my arms wildly around me in a further attempt to satisfy my debt of gratitude for the human form. This is amazing. We are amazing! I momentarily pause as I find myself in the middle of an empty road. But I have no care, I am alive. Whilst still panting slightly from my physical outburst, I look up to the skies with closed eyes and with tremendous joy bath in the warming sunshine. I feel myself smile childishly as I soak up this glorious moment. Slowly I open my eyes and observe the setting I find myself in. Even the surrounding council owned apartment blocks breathe new life into me. For they are a constant reminder of man's ingenuity and achievement as a race to have progressed and transformed from a world of wilderness and danger to one filled with the security of people's individual homes. Not habitats, but homes. Homes that then congregate to form towns and vast cities across the globe that in turn breed different societies, cultures, and ways of life. These resulting highly structured societies are complete alien concepts for all other living things on earth whose sole purpose is to expand as species. It just makes me think how incredible it is that we can now travel and have a taste of these invented and evolved civilisations by simply flying to them. Flying?! We, as two legged mammals, have mastered the skies using heavy metal machines, which upon reflection now seem implausible to me how they even stay afloat. Man's greatness truly appears to have no boundaries. We have even conquered space and time with people anywhere in the world now being able to connect and communicate with one another through a simple push of a finger on a phone or keyboard. And the ability for man to capture and retain any moment in one's journey through life in the form of a picture is just a wonderment to behold. But man's unbelievable tale of progression extends further than this. It even goes down to every object we robotically use every day with little thought, a glass, a chair, a tooth bush. Daily modern human life is truly a sign of man's desire to evolve and innovate the world around them. And as I think of this now, I have never appreciated the beauty of the human life, my life, more than in this very moment.

Bevic

Darkness surrounds me. My mind is blank and lifeless. Shit, am I dead? No, it cannot be for I can but faintly hear the escape of air from my very own breathing. My mind seems to be clouded by a thick fog of pain and discomfort. Where am I? What's going on? Fear and worry build within me. I muster just enough strength to open my eyes. Although there is light and my eyes shift side to side seeking any clue that would confirm my safety and rid me of my anxious tormenting thoughts, I cannot seem to perceive what is before me. My eyes, as if given up hope, close instinctively as discomfort surges through me. An intense burning sensation is felt over every inch of my skin as though exposed to the burning embers of a lively fire. What the fuck is this? Is this hell? I naturally twist and turn in an attempt to distinguish the discomfort. To remove these stresses currently forced upon myself by an unknown source. Momentarily I settle on myside and from the temporary rest gain enough courage to re-open my eyes in a further attempt to conceive the predicament I find myself in. A small piece of paper folded in half and residing on my briefcase confronts me. The sight of the briefcase kindles a hazy memory deep from within me. It signifies somewhat the importance it has to me, but of which I currently struggle to decipher its meaning. Am I late for work? What time is it? My thoughts trail as the level of agony arises again. Oh god, when will this ever end? Never have I felt my life in such vulnerability as I do now. It is as if my very being were on the knife's edge of ceasing to exist. Maybe this would be a better option, not existing; for living with this excruciating pain can surely not be a possibility. I subconsciously grab the paper before me and bring it closer than would normally be necessary to give myself the upmost chance of comprehending what has been written before me. In my state I can only manage to focus on the first line presented. The line seems to consist of four spidery words that I can barely make out but manage to do so; "Gone to get medicine." I let my arms drop limply, as I breathe in a sigh of relief. The Gods have answered me. I lay still. The mere knowledge that help is on the way aids in calming my thoughts. It enables me to regather the little strength required to raise my arm and finish reading the only word on the second and last line on the piece of paper; "Miro." A tidal wave of memories floods my mind, of which their origins I struggle to fully understand in nature; the horrendously seen murder, the evil yet angelical nature of the murderer himself, the briefcase holding the money stolen from an orphan organisation. The money I stole! Guilt and regret pierce my heart and soul. What have I done? What should I do now?! "Ahh." My thought processes surrender to a further surge of pain, which overshadows all other mental or physical sensations. I jerk violently side to side before once again becoming deadly still.

The beating of my own heart echoes throughout my mind; dragging me back to reality and serving as a reminder that life and blood still pump through my veins. And until it ceases to do so, I still have a hold on my destiny. I cannot stay. For as well as requiring urgent medical attention, I will not put myself in a position where there is any possibility of having to justify my actions to a man that he himself has performed indescribable acts of horror. I must leave. I must leave right now. It's the only glimmer of hope I have of rescuing myself from the dilemma I find myself in. I take a moment to brace myself for the enormous endeavour I am about to undertake. With all my might I manage to swing my legs off the bed and resume a sitting position. I feel the sweat pour of me as I find myself panting heavily with my heart beating and pumping furiously. It is as if at any moment it would break through the hard ribs protecting it, burst through the covering frail skin and onto the floor where it would then proceed to continue to beat and jump like a fish out of water. "AHH." With all my might I managed to get on my feet. I can do this! I can be free! I can leave behind all those memory demons that now follow and taunt me. All the devious acts suddenly seem worth it again. Soon enough I will give little thought to this past and instead be able to concentrate on the future. I will be able to lead a life of complete freedom and pleasure! I continue to take the next step forward into my life with this newly gained hope, whilst at the same time reaching out to the briefcase with my right hand. But the ground beneath me suddenly seems to fall away as I sense my weak and wary legs crumble under my weight. The floor rushes towards me. Once again darkness surrounds me. I have become numb. Only one physical sensation is evident to me. It is not from either the pain that the fall should have caused or even the coldness of concrete that now pushes against my bare body. It is the simple release of one tear that is almost soothing in nature as it trickles down my cheek. Why have I sacrificed myself to satisfy my greed? Impulsively, I begin to whisper out loud:

"I don't want to die...

...I don't want to die...

... I'm going to die..."

Solamov

Before exiting the car, the detective opens the glove compartment and retrieves his trusted pistol. He then proceeds to enter the apartment block and rapidly ascend the first four flights of stairs, moving up two steps at a time. As he turns the corner onto the fifth flight, he changes from grasping the pistol with one hand to both. Whilst closely hugging the wall, he begins to slowly creep upwards. From years of experience, he is breathing in smooth and controlled manner, almost mechanically in nature. He reaches the sixth floor. The detective's rhythmic motions are suddenly disrupted by a hard-slapping sound that can be heard from the ill man's room. He stands motionless, frozen solid in place. A moment of complete silence elapses. Solamov then advances to take the final step required to reach the door. He takes his handgun in his favoured right hand as he gently rests his left shoulder against the door and clutches the door handle with his remaining free hand. With the slightest of movements, he carefully confirms that the door is unlocked before lashing the door open and as quick as the blink of an eye resumes to take the pistol within both hands. It only takes the detective a short second to scan the small room and comprehend the scene played out before him. He instinctively rushes to the corner piece of his investigation, the seemingly lifeless body within the centre of the room. Panic starts to set within Solamov. The whirling abstract thoughts in his mind failing himself and Maya become ever more concrete. He hastily drops his gun as he bends down and turns the body over and, in doing so, a heavy desperate breath escapes the living corpse. Solamov's pupils instantly dilate with a sudden rush of hope. "It's okay, you are safe now." Softly speaks Solamov, as he places his arms under the body and quickly lifts him onto the bed. He knows this will be its final resting place. Whilst still panting from the physical excursion required to move the object, yet underlined with new optimism, Solamov continues to add "Listen, I am here now. I won't hurt you. Tell me what happened?" The face of the dead grimaces in pain as a few strained words are released.

"I'm sorry…briefcase…the briefcase…I'm sorry." The detective is perplexed, and fear begins to creep into his mind as the realisation becomes ever more real that he may be too late in salvaging the situation. He grabs the briefcase and places it on the body in a frantic attempt to gain allegiance with the un-living.

"Is this what you want? The briefcase?!" Solamov pronounces with rising volume into the body's un-hearing ear as he feels the investigation slip away from him in front of his very eyes. The detective's eyes shift rapidly from side to side as he tries to detect any signs of life. In his frustration and in a final effort to gain some sort of confirmation that Miroslav is the murderer, Solamov begins to furiously shake the body before him up and down using his powerful hands. The forceful vibrations cause the wooden bed posts to jutter against the solid floor. "Stay with me. Stay with me, Goddammit! Did Miroslav kill the girl?!" He pauses momentarily and holds his ear in close proximity to the mouth to listen.

"...He..." Nothing follows these words. There is only utter stillness and complete silence.

"HE? HE WHAT?!" Solamov screams in deranged state as tears start flow down his face. "JUST SAY IT! JUST SAY IT GODDAMMIT! ALL YOU HAVE TO DO IS SAY IT. DID MIROSLAV MURDER HER?!

"I did" Comes a gentle voice from behind the detective.

Miro & Solamov
"I did." The mere process of saying these two words shatters the world around me causing it to disappear into a blurry haze. No longer can I perceive my dead patient on the bed resting there with a briefcase laid upon him resembling a noble king buried with his most prized possession. He is dead. And it's all due to my lack of inactivity in helping him. I have failed him. I have killed and now I have not saved. Truly I am not worthy to stand here as I currently do, alive; inhaling this oxygen into my lungs and continue in pumping this blood through my veins. How can it be, that where another one has died, I yet live? Even the detective with a face ridden with shock and fright that one only gets from confronting death as he finds me behind him with his gun within my hands seems to fade into the background. I simply find myself staring at the pistol held within my palm. What has led me to this exact position in my life? To be standing here with a gun not knowing whether to raise it to the detective, a harmless being, or more temptingly raise it level to my temple, pull the trigger and blow this fucking brain out. This brain that has contrived disturbing thoughts and ideas and proceeded to convert them into horrifying actions. I have surely cemented my position in hell upon my death. But when will I die? When should I die? I cannot help but re-imagine the easy steps required to end this all; a slight movement upwards with my arm and the simple flex of one lousy finger to destroy me as a living being. Oh, how stupidly powerful a gun is. Power. It's difficult for me to now not reminisce that only a short while ago I myself

believed I had true power. Where I felt as if I could control not only my destiny but all those that occupy this world and worst of all, that I have the right to do so. The right to do so?! How fucking idiotic?! I sense a tear escape and run down my cheek as I now cannot comprehend or reason how I once felt so invincible and so confident in myself and the decisions I had made. And all of this I felt from slicing her throat and watching the life being drained from those beautiful sapphire blue eyes. Oh god! Forgive me! For I do not know what has led to these corrupted and poisonous thoughts?! A bullet through this diseased brain has never felt as enticing and deserving as it does now. I clench my palm around the grip in preparation for what needs to be done.

"Miroslav do not do anything silly. Put the gun down." The voice instinctively causes me to lift my head and face its source, the detective. I am brought back to reality and can re-acknowledge where I currently stand; enclosed in a small and bare concrete one room apartment. Its soulless nature accurately mirroring the events that have already unfolded within its four walls, becoming a tomb for one of its occupants. The bleakness of the setting seems to fit in perfectly with the present circumstances and potentially what is still yet to befall within it. The detective slowly rotates his body whilst keeping his eyes fixed upon mine to resume a more natural upright position. Only two meters of empty space separates the two of us as we now stand face to face. "Killing me would only exacerbate things for you." Softly speaks the Detective. I had completely forgotten that only a moment ago this was one of the two options I had presented myself. In my mind I had simply resided to the fact that the use of this ruinous tool should only be done so on those that deserve death, like me and no one else. But should I really end it all and with it completely extinguish my newly found aspirations of doing so much good in this world. To be able in some way to pay back for those lives I have cruelly and wrongly taken by helping others rebuild and value theirs.

*

Panic starts to set in Solamov as his words elicit no definable response from the man before him. In a final attempt to convince the young man not to become his executioner, "Look, back-up is on its way and from how I see it, friend, you can do one of two things. You can either shoot me or flee. But I will guarantee my colleagues will make your life a living hell when they catch you. And they will catch you. Or you can sensibly put down the gun and do the right thing and turn yourself in. You are young; with cooperation and good behaviour you will be back out before you are fifty. Make the right choice friend."

*

Who does this guy think he is?! 'Backup'?! 'Friend?!' As if he has the arrogance to try and manipulate me. Me?! A man that fully understands the incredible nature of the human mind. What sort of ignorant fool stands before me?! For does he not know what I am capable of? Does he not realise the intense misery that I have thrust upon others with ease and the precarious position he has now put himself in? How and why should one live that is so stupidly senseless?! Almost subconsciously I can feel my right arm extend outwards and raise the gun.

*

"Tell me detective, do you not appreciate life?"

"I do." He responds after visibly swallowing as he now looks straight down the barrel of the gun.

"But do you really detective?" questions Miroslav sternly. "For have you ever acknowledged how truly amazing the human life is? How at certain times in one's life one can feel such anguish and despair and yet in another moment within that same passage of life one can feel so indescribably elated by the offerings that life has to give?" No answer was forth coming. Only the sharp deep inhalations and exhalations by the two men can now be heard within the room. In. out. In. out. "Do you realise...?" he pauses as his face crunches up in distress to fight away the inevitable tears that are to follow. "Detective, do you realise, do realise how beautiful life is?! And yet, how fucking fragile it is?! DO YOU?!" screams Miroslav forcefully. He does this whilst making several pointing motions directly towards the detective with the gun held within his shaking outstretched arm as to reinforce the point he has just made.

The eyes of the two men fix upon one another. A moment passes. A serene peaceful silence fills the room as both men enter a state of deep self-thought. One contemplates his life whilst the other his death. The situation is perfectly imbalanced. One man considers what has passed and what has led him to where he currently stands. The other reflects on the real possibility of his death and what would become of him in the future if this were not to emerge as an actuality. Though unaware to each other their thoughts do find common ground. They both begin to believe they have comprehended the present and that their life, right now, is in the hands of the other. "I am sorry detective." Solamov straightens his back, tenses every muscle of his body, and closes his eyes for slightly longer than a standard blink to ready himself for what he deems is certain to follow. "But this time the choice of life or death resides with you." With a sudden swift flick of Miro's wrist, the pistol travels the short distance to Solamov who impulsively catches it within his chest. In a flash the detective has the gun clutched within his favoured right hand and has it pointing at Miro.

Only now as Solamov has the gun directed at the murderer does his mind actually have the time to consider what has just played out before him. A moment ago he could not have been more confident that he was experiencing his last few seconds on this earth. The appreciation that this was not the case was fleeting. His attention overridden by the choice now given to him by the killer. "I am not going to jail. No one will carry the burden heavier for what I have done than myself. It has happened and cannot be undone, but I have truly learnt from it. I give you my word, for that is all I can give, that if you allow me to be free, I will now go on to live a life of virtue and kindness." Utters Miro in soft and relaxed manner, for he is now relieved of the pressure that no longer resides upon him. "A life of freedom or death. Those are the only two choices that I present to you and that I am willing to accept."

"It's more choice than Anna got" declares the detective. Each word spoken with an undercurrent of rage and disgust. Miro briefly lowers his gaze before resuming to stare directly at his judicator with eyes filled with pain and self-loathing. This is contrary to those of the judicator, the detective, whose eyes only emit anger. The source of this anger that is swirling and building within the depths of Solamov is not from what one might expect it to be. It comes more from his own acknowledgment that he does not know what to do. And for a man that prides himself on his decisiveness and his ability to make the right choice whenever he has been called on do so, this situation of complete ambivalence is the highest form of frustration. An endless series of thoughts flow through the detective's structured mind; always with different beginnings but forever resulting in the same disciplined question. Redeem the death of Anna, a young innocent girl with so much life ahead of her; but do I, Dmitry Solamov, have the right to kill a defenceless man. To uphold the promises made to the grieving mother of the slaughtered daughter and with it brings a certain level of justice to the world; but do I, Dmitry Solamov, have the right to kill a defenceless man.

To shoot a bullet through this coldblooded murderer's brain; but do I, Dmitry Solamov, have the right to kill a defenceless man.

*

"Goodbye Detective." I turn to face the open door and the corridor beyond. I take a step forward into my new life. A life that I vow to myself right now will be one filled with only kindness and with deeds of compassion to those that require it. Although I have killed and not saved, I will do everything in my power to bring happiness and comfort to people in need of it. And if I am able to make even one person appreciate their life more and the real beauty that life is, I will truly be on the path to redemption. Surely this is the purpose of not only my life but life in general; to do good upon others. All of a sudden, my chest violently and unnaturally jolts upwards before the sound reaches and deafens my ears. All the air trapped within my lungs is expelled as I struggle to carry on breathing. The second bullet, just like the first, causes my body to jerk atypically as it tears through me with little hindrance. I impulsively place my right hand behind my back in a weird desperate attempt that if I can establish the source of this paralysis maybe I could reverse its effects. Whilst undergoing this futile activity I turn, slowly, back into the room. I stumble one step but manage momentarily to regain my composure before subsequently unwillingly falling upon my knees. Defeatedly my arms drop limp to my side. But it's not yet the end. Not while I still have some energy. I manage to raise my gaze to look before me at the servant of the law who has become a fallen angel. Is he any better than me, for he has also killed? Does he deserve to live on? Through the fallen-one's leg I can see the remains of a man who was as much killed by his own greed as he was by me not saving him. But did he deserve to die? Do I deserve to? This cannot be my last thought. I will not let this be my last thought! I close my eyes and raise my head to the sky. As though I was listening to a gentle beautiful melody, I sense a soft smile tiptoe across my face. What an incredible and truly magnificent life I have led? It has truly been a great honour to have lived and to have experienced all of life's emotions: power, elation, depression, rage, boundless regret, unnatural levels of hope and determination, the deepest of appreciation for life, and most importantly of course, I have witnessed unparalleled beauty; her beauty. Oh, how dreadfully stunning her sapphire blue eyes were?

END

Printed in Great Britain
by Amazon